Eloise's Summer Vacation

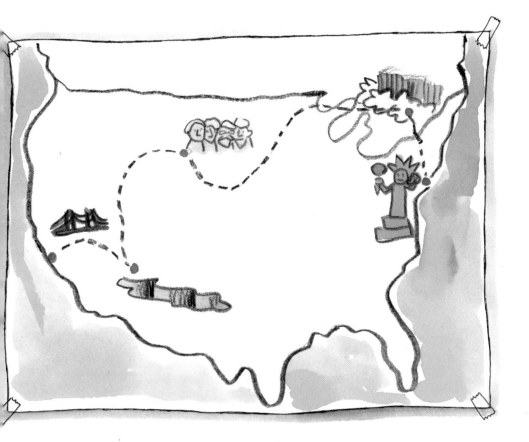

KAY THOMPSON'S ELOISE

Eloise's Summer Vacation

WITHDRAWN

STORY BY Lisa McClatchy

ILLUSTRATED BY Tammie Lyon

Ready-to-Read

Simon Spotlight
New York   London   Toronto   Sydney   New Delhi

SIMON SPOTLIGHT
An imprint of Simon & Schuster Children's Publishing Division
1230 Avenue of the Americas, New York, NY 10020
First Simon Spotlight hardcover edition May 2017
First Aladdin Paperbacks edition May 2007
For information about special discounts for bulk purchases, please contact Simon & Schuster
Special Sales at 1-866-506-1949 or business@simonandschuster.com.
The text of this book was set in Century Old Style.
Manufactured in the United States of America 0417 LAK
2 4 6 8 10 9 7 5 3 1
Library of Congress Control Number 2006933268
ISBN 978-1-4814-8820-4 (hc)
ISBN 978-0-689-87454-3 (pbk)

"Eloise,"
Nanny says,
"it is time to pack!"

Nanny and I
are going on vacation.
I know just what to bring!

This is the Butler.
He is also the driver.

Nanny sits up front.
She has her own TV.

Weenie and I try to sit.
Sometimes we do.

Sometimes we don't.
"Stay in your seats!"
Nanny says.

"First stop!"
says the Butler.

"Niagara Falls!" I say.

Weenie and I
like the spray.

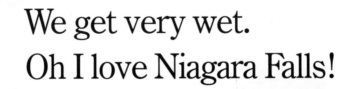

We get very wet.
Oh I love Niagara Falls!

Being on the road is fun.
I brush Nanny's hair.

I brush Weenie's hair.

I try to brush
the Butler's hair.
"No, no, no!" says Nanny.

"Next stop!"
says the Butler.
"Mount Rushmore!"
I say.

I take my art supplies.
Nanny and the Butler pose.

Nanny looks like Lincoln.
So does the Butler.
Oh I love Mount Rushmore.

"Third stop!"
says the Butler.

"The Grand Canyon!"
I say.

Nanny wants to hike
on foot.
I prefer donkeys.

So does Weenie.
The Butler prefers
to nap.

We win.
We ride to the bottom.
Oh I love the Grand Canyon!

"Last stop!"
says the Butler.
"San Francisco!"
I say.

"To the hotel!" says Nanny.
"To the hotel!"
    says the Butler.

"Do they have room service?" I say.

Oh I love,
love, love vacation!